CHAIR-ISH THE THOUGHT

TRASH TO TREASURE COZY MYSTERIES, BOOK 2

DONNA CLANCY

SUMMER PRESCOTT BOOKS PUBLISHING

To my mom, I miss you so much.

CHAPTER ONE

"This is exciting," Gabby said, climbing into her friend's van. "I've never been to a storage auction before."

"It is fun, most of the time. Sometimes the people who are bidding get testy when they lose a unit they really want. I've actually seen fistfights break out," Sage said, starting the van.

"Let's not get involved in anything like that, okay?"

"Believe me, I stay as far away from those kinds of people as possible."

"I see the van is empty. Are you expecting to win a few bids today?"

"You never know. Sometimes the units are loaded with furniture and other times not so much. You can't go into the unit or touch or move anything. You have to bid on just what you can see from the door and if I see items I can flip, I will bid."

"Rory gave me some money in case I see tools or fishing poles. You know, the things he always wants me to find for him. I'm looking for craft or holiday stuff for myself."

"Most times there is Christmas stuff in the units. Maybe you'll find something you like."

Moosehead Storage was located on the far side of Moosehead. The business conducted a semiannual auction to clear out units that had been abandoned by their owners or the monthly fees had not been paid for a consecutive three-month period. Gabby was on their email list so she would be told in advance when the auction was going to be held and how many units would be for sale.

"Do you want to stop for a coffee? We do have a little extra time as we are only ten minutes away and the auction doesn't start until ten," Sage asked. "My stomach just growled."

"Is that the gosh-awful noise I just heard?" Gabby asked. "We'd better stop. I don't want you passing out in the summer sun from lack of food."

They pulled into the *Sip and Dip* a mile up the road from the storage facility. As the two friends discussed whether to sit in the restaurant or take their food to go, a loud commotion broke out in front of them. They moved closer to see what was going on at the register.

"I said cream and sugar in my coffee, not black," the man said, yelling at the clerk and slamming down a coffee cup in his hand. "How can you screw up a simple order like that?"

"I'm sorry. I'll get you a new cup," she said, visibly shaken from his demanding attitude.

"That's right, you will. And I expect a couple of free donuts to make up for your stupidity," he yelled as she hurried off to get the new coffee.

"What a jerk," Sage said a little too loud.

The man turned and advanced toward her.

"You have a problem with me, little girl?" he asked, getting right in her face.

"Yea, I do," Sage answered, not being one to back down. "You're a jerk!"

He grabbed her by the arm trying to intimidate her. Instead, he just made her angrier.

"Get your hand off me, or you will regret it," she stated in a low, throaty voice.

"I'm so scared," he said, laughing and tightening his grip.

Sage had had enough. She stomped on the top of

his foot with all her might. He let out a yelp, and she could see the pain on his face. At that point, the owner had come out from the kitchen and threw the man out. He limped to his truck listening to the other customers laughing at him as he left. He apologized to Gabby and Sage and told them their coffee and whatever else they wanted was on the house.

"Nice move," Gabby said as they waited for their order.

"Sometimes the money I spent on self-defense classes pays off," Sage said, leaving a good-sized tip in the jar for the rattled clerk.

"Let's hope we don't run into him again," Gabby said. "He wasn't very pleasant."

"I've never seen him before, but then again, Moosehead has a lot bigger population than Cupston does. Are you ready? We are behind schedule now and will get there with just enough time to register before the sale begins."

The friends hurried into the office to register for the bidding. They each got a number and headed out to join the crowd that was waiting for the gates to open. The auctioneer gave his usual spiel, and the gates opened.

The first two units had nothing that interested either Sage or Gabby, so they watched while the other bidders fought over the units. The third unit was opened, and Sage immediately knew she had to win it.

It was packed with furniture and various household items that she could use in her flipping business. Sage played her flashlight over the items in the unit trying to see what was in the rear section behind the obvious things they could see up front.

"Check out that wing-back Victorian chair in the back corner. It looks to be in good shape and could bring three hundred dollars when it sells. I can see at least three different beds on the side in front of it. This unit is a goldmine for me. I hope the bidding doesn't go too high," Sage said, walking away from the door so others could look in before the bidding started.

"Let's begin," the auctioneer said. "Who will give me fifty dollars?"

"Three hundred dollars," someone yelled from the back of the crowd.

Everyone turned to see who the bidder was, and Gabby grabbed Sage's arm when they saw who it was. He glared at Sage as their eyes met.

"Three fifty," Sage countered.

"I have three fifty. Do I hear four?"

"Four hundred," he yelled.

"Four fifty," Sage said, not backing down.

"Five hundred," he countered before the auctioneer could even say anything.

"Six hundred," Sage yelled.

"That's a lot of money," Gabby whispered to her friend.

"I can make five times that when I'm done flipping everything," she whispered back. "That unit is packed to the gills."

"I have six hundred. Do I hear seven hundred?"

The guy bidding against Sage punched the door of the locker he was standing next to. He hurried away, not uttering a word or looking back. Jumping into his truck he peeled out of the parking lot, almost hitting another car.

"I have six hundred. Going once, going twice, sold to the lady in the purple baseball cap."

"It's more than I wanted to spend on one unit, but it is a good one. It probably would have gone for a lot less if it hadn't been for that guy bidding me up."

"He was extremely mad when he left here," Gabby replied.

"That's his problem. Let's lock this up and keep going," Sage said, putting her own padlock on the unit door.

Two units later Gabby scored a smaller unit that

had everything she was looking for in it. She was so excited when her winning bid was only fifty dollars. Sage could see that her best friend had caught the auction bug and would be going to auctions with her in the future.

Sage was careful bidding the rest of the day as she basically knew how much would fit in her van. She scored two more smaller units that had a little bit of furniture but mostly boxes that she had no idea what they contained and wouldn't know until after the auction was over.

At the auction's conclusion, the two friends went into the office to pay for their units, and then pulled the van up in front of the one filled with furniture. Gabby pulled the items out of the space and set them next to the rear door. Sage loaded the van fitting everything together like puzzle pieces in a finished puzzle.

"Oh, what a shame," Gabby said, coming out of the unit carrying the wing-back chair and setting it down next to Sage. "There's a tear on the front of it. A computer tower was put on top of it and the metal corner made a slit in the material."

"That's not bad. It can be fixed, and if it can't, I'll reupholster it. It's still in great shape for its age," Sage said, examining the tear.

"How old do you think it is?"

"This chair is from the turn of the twentieth century. Someone took very good care of it along with most of the furniture in here. I made a major score with this unit," Sage said, happily.

Four hours later, the van was packed so full that the final boxes were placed on the floor under Gabby's feet and balanced on the console between the two seats. Gabby crawled up into her seat and hooked up her seatbelt before Sage placed the final box in her lap for the ride home.

"So, when is the next auction?" Gabby asked.

"I knew you were hooked. I could see it on your face when you won your unit," Sage said, laughing. "There's one next month up in Lewiston. I was planning on going, but usually when I go to that one, I go up and stay the night before. Let me know if you're in."

"I'm in. Just give me the date so I can make sure my schedule is clear at the salon. Speaking of the salon, you didn't forget you have an appointment next week, did you?"

"It's on my calendar."

Gabby Rhodes opened her own salon, *Cut Ups*, after she graduated beauty school. The salon had started small with Gabby being the only stylist, but now she had three other hairdressers working for her. She was a natural when it came to cutting and styling hair, and the salon had an outstanding reputation and had been featured in many hair design magazines.

Sage on the other hand couldn't wait to graduate from high school and be done with studying. She also had a natural ability; to find beauty in junk. Flipping furniture and different odds and ends since she was a young teen, she had redone her own bedroom using all her early projects. Many of her flipped items were sold in her mom's shop, *This and That.* She also had a large online following.

"When we get back to Cupston I'll drop you off at your house. Your boxes are all mixed in with mine so when I empty the van, I'll put your stuff back in and bring it over to your house in the morning. Is that agreeable?"

"I can't wait to show Rory what I got for fifty bucks," Gabby said, smiling. "He's going to love that box of old tools that was tucked in the back of the unit."

"He's going to have to build himself a small museum to show off all the tools he has accumulated," Sage replied.

"You know I try not to be a worrywart, right?" Gabby asked.

"Yeah, why?"

"I've been watching in the side mirror, and I believe the guy that bid against you has been following us."

Sage tried to see out the driver's side mirror who was behind them, but the vehicle was staying on the edge of the road rather than the middle. Her van was so packed, the rearview mirror was useless.

"Can you get a license plate number?" Sage asked.

"I'll try," Gabby said, keeping watch in the mirror.

"I don't want him following us all the way home. I'm going to pull into Fulton Farm unless I can…" she said. "Hold on to the box in your lap."

Sage started tapping the brakes. She wanted the guy behind them to know that they knew he was there. After several minutes of hitting the brakes, the van had slowed to almost twenty miles an hour from the forty-five they had been going. The truck flew out around them and took off up the road.

"I got the license plate," Gabby stated, pulling paper and pen out of her purse to write it down.

"I think I'm going to pull into the farm anyway and call Sheriff White from there. I don't know if that guy will be waiting for us somewhere farther up the road, and I don't want to take a chance."

A short time later, they pulled into the parking lot at Fulton Farm. They looked around the area before exiting the van. Sage pulled out her cell and called the station requesting the sheriff meet them there.

"I told the sheriff we would meet him at the farm stand," Sage said. "They have some terrific premade salads there made with all the produce grown on the farm. I don't know about you, but I'm hungry."

"Lead the way. Maybe Cliff is there," Gabby said, teasing her friend.

Cliff Fulton was the twenty-eight-year-old son of the owners, Shirley and Pierce Fulton. Sage agreed to go out on one date with him after going through a bad breakup with her former boyfriend and not dating for over a year. Now the two were spending a lot of time together, and Sage was so glad she had said yes to their first date. He was good looking, extremely smart, and fun to be with. He made Sage laugh, which was very important to her. And it helped that her mom liked him, too.

"Hey, good looking," Cliff said as they entered the building.

"I'm sure you're talking to me, right?" Gabby replied, batting her eyes.

"Of course I am," he replied, laughing. "Who else would I be talking to?"

"Oh, I don't know," Gabby answered, walking away toward the refrigerators.

"What's happening? I never see you in the middle of the day," he asked.

Sage explained the meeting with the gruff man at the coffee shop and then how she outbid him on a locker he seemed to really want. She told Cliff that they had sidetracked here because he was following them, and she didn't want to lead him right to her house.

"You were smart stopping here," he agreed. "I'll go out and take a look around to see if I can spot a truck with someone sitting in it."

"A white, beat-up truck," Sage yelled as he went out the door.

Sage was watching Cliff out the door when the sheriff's cruiser pulled into the parking lot. She went outside to meet with him while Gabby kept shopping. She explained again what happened and gave him the piece of paper with the license plate number and description of the truck written on it. He told her to be careful and that he would check out who this guy was and get back to her.

Sage and Cliff returned to the farm stand to find

Gabby standing at the register with a full hand basket waiting to check out. At the side of the basket was a salad that she had originally come in for.

"Look at the size of these tomatoes," she exclaimed, holding up a beefsteak variety. "I can make three sandwiches out of this one alone. There's nothing like a fresh tomato sandwich loaded with mayo, salt, and pepper."

"That's the first batch of the season," Cliff said. "We have some great crops coming in this year."

"I can't wait for apple picking season. I love the pressed apple cider and cider donuts that you produce here," Sage stated. "I usually buy enough donuts to freeze some so I can enjoy them through the winter."

"We never have any leftovers for me to freeze," Cliff said chuckling. "I guess that means I'll have to come to your house for some."

"Nothing like being obvious," Gabby said, rolling her eyes as she emptied her basket's contents onto the counter. "I didn't grab you a salad because I didn't know what kind you wanted. There's like eight different kinds to pick from."

"That's fine. I'll grab my own, and maybe we can stay here and eat our late lunch out at the picnic tables. I'm going to grab a water; do you want one?"

"Please. That's one thing I forgot to get," Gabby replied.

The three friends sat at a table near the stand door so Cliff could go inside if customers entered the building. They soon forgot about the guy following them and enjoyed their lunch in the warm, summer sun. They finished eating and went inside to say goodbye to Cliff who had returned to the register to ring out several customers. He told Sage he would see her at her mother's shop in the morning as he had some items to drop off that his mother wanted to place on consignment there.

"I think it's just another excuse to see you again," Gabby whispered as they exited the building. "His mother could bring the stuff over herself on Wednesday when your mom is there."

"As much as you like to tease me, I do enjoy spending time with Cliff, so I don't mind his excuses to see me," Sage said. "Now, let's get you home."

It was late afternoon when Sage pulled into her own driveway. She stood at the back of the van trying to decide whether or not to unload it then or in the morning. Tuesday was her day to work at her mother's shop, *This and That,* so Sarah could have a full day off.

After the last break-in Sage had her workshop

fitted with an alarm system. Making her mind up that the items would be safer in her shop than in her old van, she started to unload the day's purchases. Walking back and forth she was trying to figure why the gruff man wanted the unit so badly. It was just a bunch of old furniture as far as Sage could tell.

Although everything fit in the shop, Sage knew she would have to move the bigger pieces to her new storage trailer in the near future if she wanted to have any room to work. She set the alarm, slipped out the door, and locked it before the alarm engaged.

Passing on supper because of eating lunch later than usual, Sage grabbed a beer and went to sit out on her back deck in the warm evening. Lighting a citronella bucket to keep the mosquitoes away, she plopped into the hammock, rocking herself with one foot that was extended to the wooden floor. She closed her eyes and listened to the crickets and tree frogs as they sang their songs in the dark night.

She loved Maine because of moments like this one. Yes, the winters could be long and harsh, but it was worth it. Cupston was a quaint town with a small population, and as such, houses were not built on top of each other, which would make it easy to peer into your neighbor's windows. The closest house to Sage's was almost a quarter of a mile away, and that was how she liked it, peaceful and quiet.

Her place was a small farmhouse, almost a hundred years old. It had character to it like the large fireplace and hearth with the built-in bread oven that graced her living room. The ceilings were low, as that was how the houses had been built back then to keep the heat in and circulating. She even had a fireplace in her bedroom. A large cellar that had been used in the past for storing canned food and winter rations was hardly ever visited by Sage. The dirt floor wasn't the best place to store things. During the spring months, the cellar would flood because of the melting snow.

The house had been a graduation gift from her father. Not being around for much of her life, he wanted to make up for it by making sure she would always have a place to live. He also made sure it had a large, double garage that she could turn into a workshop. Not having a mortgage to pay was a huge step in Sage being able to go into business for herself. Now, nine years later, her business was thriving, and she was enjoying a comfortable life at her young age.

Samuel Fletcher lived in the next town over in Meadows Falls. Father and daughter spoke on a regular basis but were not as close as Sage was to her mother. Her father had remarried after her parents' divorce, but Sage didn't really know his new wife, Ina, since they had only met a handful of times over the last nine years.

Sage's mind fluttered back to the events of the afternoon. She couldn't remember if she had locked her front door and got up to check it. The house was in complete darkness because she had been out back on the deck. As she reached the front door, a shrill noise broke the quiet of the night. The alarm was going off in her workshop, and she knew just who it was that was trying to break in.

CHAPTER TWO

Grabbing her cell out of her back pocket, she called the police station to report a break-in in progress. Then she grabbed her metal bat that she kept next to the front door in an umbrella stand and headed out to her workshop. She slowly approached the shop, bat poised above her head. A vehicle engine roared to life out on the road and sped away. A minute later, a cruiser coming from the opposite direction with its lights flashing sped into her driveway.

Sage unlocked the door and disabled the alarm. Deputy Andy Bell pulled out his flashlight and entered the workshop to make sure no one was secreted in there. He gave an all clear and returned outside.

"I don't think he even got inside," Sage said.

"He?"

"Yeah, I believe it was the guy from the auction today that was mad because I outbid him for a unit. He attempted to follow us home, but we ducked into Fulton Farm. When we came out, he wasn't around. The Sheriff met us there and took a report and plate number we got on the truck."

"Oh, yeah, that's the plate I ran this afternoon. The truck had been stolen from Portland earlier this week," Bell said.

"I guess he needed a truck to move whatever it was he wanted in the unit today," Sage replied. "He had to register a name to bid in the auction. Maybe the sheriff could call the storage facility and find out what name he used."

"If he stole the truck, I'm sure he used an assumed name at the auction," Bell said.

"You're probably right," Sage said, sighing. "I wonder what is so important in this unit that he wants. I'm almost afraid to go to work at my mom's shop tomorrow. With no one here all day, I'm sure he will attempt to get in my workshop again whether the alarm goes off or not. This is one of those rare times I wish my neighbors were a little closer than they are."

"Does your alarm system have a camera attached?" Bell asked, surveying the area.

"Yes, it does, but I'm sure that a camera won't faze him because both Gabby and I have already seen his face, along with everyone at the donut shop and the storage facility."

"We can make a few passes during the day, but that's all that I can promise we can do."

"I think I'm going to call my mom and see if she will change her day off to Wednesday. Then I can go through everything that was in the unit tomorrow in the daylight. I might even ask Cliff to come over for a few hours, so I have a male presence here with me."

"Good idea. I heard through the grapevine that you and Cliff were a thing now," Bell said, smiling.

"A thing? Right now, it's just two friends enjoying each other's company," Sage replied.

"I don't think so. That's not the way Cliff looks at it according to his mom."

"Did you hear it directly from his mom or through the town gossip vine?"

"You got me, town gossip vine," he admitted.

"Just as I thought. Are we done here? I need to go in and call my mom to check on tomorrow," Sage asked.

"I'll stay here until you alarm the shop again and

you get inside. Call if he returns, and do me a favor, don't go outside to face him alone. If this guy is as bad as you say he is, he wouldn't hesitate to turn the bat on you."

"I'll stay inside, I promise," Sage said, setting the alarm and locking the door for a second time. "Thanks, Andy. Have a good night."

Sage watched the cruiser pull away and pulled out her cell phone. She called her mother to tell her what was going on, but Sarah already knew. She had run in to Gabby at the grocery store, and she had told her everything. Her mom agreed to swap her day to Wednesday but insisted that her daughter call Cliff to see if he could spend at least part of the day with her.

Her next phone call was to Cliff who agreed to be at her house at eight in the morning. He had to return to the farm around noon since he was scheduled to restock the farm stand in the afternoon. She told him she'd have the coffee on when he got there.

Sage didn't sleep well that night. The house didn't have an alarm system since she'd never had the need for one before now. Her bedroom was on the second floor, and it looked out over the workshop. She kept her window open about an inch so she could hear if anything moved outside in her yard. Sage finally dozed off as the sun was coming up, and the alarm clock on her phone sounded shortly after that. She was exhausted.

Half a pot of coffee had already been consumed by Sage before Cliff even got there. He arrived with a dozen donuts.

"Not trying to sound nasty or anything, but you look awful," Cliff said, pouring himself a mug of coffee.

"I didn't sleep much last night.," she replied, biting into a honey-dip donut. "Yum! These are still warm."

"Only way to eat them," he said, grabbing a donut out of the box. "So, what are we looking for today?"

"I don't know. It has to be something valuable. Otherwise, why would this guy take so many chances to get whatever it is?"

"Sounds right. Shall we get to it?"

Sage disarmed the security system and swung open the two doors to the shop. Cliff whistled when he saw how much stuff was crammed into the work area. She explained that the larger pieces were eventually going to be put out in the trailer to free up her space to work. He suggested she go unlock it, and as they went through the furniture, he would take it out to the trailer once the piece had been checked.

"I'll start on this end," Cliff said.

They chattered as they went through everything piece by piece looking for hidden compartments. Sage carefully peeled back a paper backing on a painting and found five hundred dollars in older fifty-dollar bills hidden between the canvas and the backing.

"Well, this alone has almost covered what I paid for the whole unit," she said, smiling.

"We better check all the paintings I have already put aside," Cliff replied. "Maybe I'll start going to auctions with you."

"Gabby already got the bug. Wait until she finds out about the money hidden in the painting."

Sage checked the paintings already put aside and found more hidden cash. She reached the Victorian wing-back and moved the computer tower to access the damage to the chair. She threw the tower out the door and it landed on the driveway with a loud crash.

"How do you know that there's not something important on the computer memory and that's not what this guy is after?" Cliff asked.

"I never thought of that," she said, retrieving the tower and setting it under her work bench. "At least it didn't do much damage to the chair. I think I can fix it without too much trouble."

She ran her hand along the material of the chair

looking for anything lumpy or that did not belong there. Removing the cushion, she repeated her search on the seat of the chair.

A car approached the garage, and the two stopped working and turned around to see who it was. Sheriff White exited his personal vehicle and walked up to them sporting a serious look.

"Bad news?" Sage asked, seeing his face. "Would a cup of coffee help?"

"It wouldn't hurt," he replied.

"So why so glum?" Sage asked, returning with a mug of black coffee for the sheriff.

"I called Moosehead PD and requested they go see what name the suspect used on his auction registration form. When they arrived there to question the owner, the office was in a shambles, and they couldn't find Sam Morrison anywhere even though his car was there."

"Please tell me they found him," Sage said.

"They did, but it wasn't good. He was beaten up pretty bad and left in the dumpster outside the office. If the police hadn't got there when they did, he might have died. He's in the hospital under police guard and is expected to recover completely."

"He went back to get my address. That's how he

knew where I lived and was able to show up here last night," Sage said, frowning.

"Have you found anything valuable enough to warrant his behavior?"

"We've found some cash hidden behind some paintings, but it didn't amount to enough to beat someone up for," Cliff replied.

"How much is some?" the sheriff asked.

"So far, almost two grand in fifties," Cliff answered. "But we haven't finished yet."

"To someone with nothing, that kind of money might be a huge motivator," the sheriff said.

"But how would he know the money was even there unless it was his unit to begin with?" Cliff asked.

"With the office in a shambles, we can't even find out who originally owned the unit," Sage replied. "If we could find that out, it might give us a clue as to what we are looking for."

"I have to get to the station. Thanks for the coffee," he said, handing back the empty mug. "Sage, be careful. This guy means business."

"I may be sleeping on the couch until this guy is caught," Cliff suggested.

"Not a bad idea," the sheriff replied before climbing in his car and driving away.

The couple returned to the task at hand. Sage stood there staring at the chair.

"Did you find something?"

"No, it's just the more I look at this chair the more I like it. I don't have much furniture in my bedroom, and this might look good sitting next to the window. I could put a patch on the tear cut from the matching underneath material. It wouldn't be as perfect as I would need to make it for resale, but it would be good enough for my own bedroom."

"Hey, sometimes you have to do something for yourself. Do you want me to carry it up to your room for you?"

"That would be awesome. My room is the first door on the right at the top of the stairs."

They had only got through half the items before Cliff had to leave for work.

"Did you mean what you said about sleeping here tonight?" Sage asked, hesitantly. "You wouldn't have to sleep on the couch. I do have a spare room with a double bed."

"I did and I would rather sleep downstairs in case this idiot is able to get in the house," Cliff replied. "I get off work at six, and I'll be back then."

"I'll have some supper ready for when you get

here," Sage offered. "Chicken on the grill sound okay?"

"Sounds good. I'll bring some squash and tomatoes from the stand to go with it. Please be careful after I leave. I would rather you lock up the shop and stay inside the house."

"I can't do that. I need to finish going through the stuff because I have to work at *This and That* tomorrow and won't be around in case he breaks in while I'm gone. I have to do my best to find whatever it is before he can get his hands on it."

"Do me a favor and at least put all the cash in the house before I leave. At least that won't be a tease to him if he does show up and sees it lying on the workbench."

"I'll be right back," Sage said, scooping up the money and running to the house.

She walked him to his truck when she returned. He took her hands and gave her a quick kiss on the cheek. This wasn't the first time he had done anything like that, but Sage could still feel herself blushing.

"Please be extra careful," he said.

"I promise. I'll see you after work."

She watched him drive away and returned to the task at hand. Her mind kept wandering to what Andy had said, wondering if there was some truth to the gossip after what Cliff had just done when he left. It had been a few months since their first date and maybe he wanted to take their relationship up a notch and for her to be his girlfriend. She didn't know if she was ready or not as she didn't want to rush into things after her break-up with Perry.

Get your mind on your work and off your social life.

Sage found another couple hundred dollars hidden here and there along with some old jewelry that she was sure was from the late 1800s or early 1900s. It looked like costume jewelry but very well made. Her mother knew more about antique jewelry than she did. Sage would give the pieces to her mother to sell in her shop.

After going over everything that she'd taken out of the unit at the auction, she found nothing that was valuable enough for someone to almost kill for it. The next hour was spent moving some of the larger pieces to the storage trailer. Each time she returned from the backyard, she would glance around the area making sure no one was nearby and ready to pounce.

Five o'clock rolled around. Sage set the alarm and locked the shop. Returning to her house, she planned to take a shower and then start supper. Standing in the stream of hot water, she thought she heard a bang coming from downstairs. She listened but heard nothing further. Wrapping herself in a towel, she exited the bathroom to find herself face to face with the man from the auction. He was in the process of picking up her wingback chair and attempting to take off with it.

She let out a scream and ran for the bat standing in the corner of her bedroom. He dropped the chair and came after her. He grabbed the bat and tried to twist it out of her hand. Sage countered by taking one hand off the bat and driving the heel of her hand into his nose with all her might.

He let out a wail and released his hold on the bat. Sage took the opportunity to kick him in the knee which she could hear snap as she made the connection. He limped out of the room as best he could. Threatening her, he promised that she wouldn't be so lucky when he returned. He left a trail of blood that was pouring out of his nose as he ran down the stairs. She heard the screen door bang at the back of the house, and then she watched him out of her bedroom window as he ran down the driveway.

She called 911, and the dispatcher promised to send someone right out.

"At least I know what he is after now," she said,

walking over to the chair. "What is so important about this specific piece of furniture?"

Taking a flashlight out of her nightstand, she pulled on the hole in the material at the front of the chair to look inside. There was nothing to be seen. Tipping the chair over so she could peruse the bottom, she cut a small swatch of material out of the lining that she knew she would use to fix the front of the chair. Shining the flashlight in the hole she had created; she saw something that had been tied to the frame of the chair.

Her pulse quickened, and her breath came quicker. She enlarged the hole by a few more inches so she could get her hand inside. Grabbing onto the twine that attached the small package to the frame, she found the knot and pulled it. It didn't budge. She tried again, and this time it loosened a little. The third time was a charm, and the twine fell loose allowing the small package to release from the frame.

Sage pulled the item out of the chair. It was a small brown box, two inches by two inches. There was no writing on it and when she shook it, there was no sound from within. She carefully opened the cover. A small velvet satchel was folded neatly inside.

Not wanting to drop anything, she took the velvet bag to her bed and sat down. The ribbons opened easily, and Sage turned the bag upside down and shook it. Inhaling deeply when she saw what had fallen out, she sat there staring in amazement at what was in front of her.

"Sage! Where are you? Are you okay?" Sheriff White yelled from the first floor.

"I'm up here. First door on the right. You won't believe what I found," she replied.

CHAPTER THREE

"Whose blood is on the stairs? Please tell me it's not yours. Do I need to call an ambulance?" he yelled as he rushed to the bedroom door.

"I'm fine, but I can't say the same for the guy from the auction. He might have a broken nose and probably a busted knee," Sage replied.

"Using those self-defense courses again," he said, chuckling. "Good for you."

"I found what he was after. Come check this out," she said, pointing to the bed.

"Do you think you might want to get dressed before anyone else shows up?" the sheriff asked from the doorway. "Like Cliff?"

In the excitement of the moment, Sage had forgotten that she was sitting there with just a towel wrapped around herself. The towel that had been wrapped around her wet hair had fallen off in the tussle, and her hair was unbrushed and sticking up everywhere.

"You have to see this first."

The sheriff walked to the bed and let out a whistle. Sitting on the purple comforter was a small pile of glittering diamonds.

"There're twenty-one of them. Looking at them, I would estimate that they range from half a carat to almost two carats," she said. "Stand guard over them while I get dressed."

She disappeared into the bathroom and returned fully clothed with her hair brushed in its normal style. The sheriff was scrutinizing the diamonds like he was looking for something.

"How did you find them?" he asked.

"I came out of the bathroom to see Mr. Personality trying to leave with my chair. I knew whatever it was he was looking for had to be secreted somewhere in the chair. I cut a couple of holes and found a box secured to the underneath frame of the chair."

"How did he know the chair was up here?"

"Either he watched Cliff carry it inside from the shop, or he could see it in the window from the driveway," Sage replied. "I'm kind of glad Cliff is staying here tonight. This guy was really furious when he left. He threatened he'd be back and that I'd be sorry."

"We definitely have to find out who the owner of the storage unit was," the sheriff stated. "Although looking at these diamonds I would venture to say they are well over a hundred years old."

"Why do you think they are that old?" Sage asked, picking one up.

"There is no laser identification on any of the diamonds, and they look like they were cut by hand."

"A laser identification?"

"Starting in the 1980s, lasers were used to burn identification numbers into the diamonds to be able to track them. And these are rough cut, by hand. If they were cut by current day machines, they would be a lot smoother and more evenly cut."

"And how do you know so much about diamonds?" Sage asked.

"My mother, God rest her soul, was a jewelry appraiser. She taught me quite a bit about gems and especially diamonds; they were her specialty. Her expertise was sought out often, and she was well respected in her field."

"That is so interesting. So do you think these diamonds have been hidden in that chair for a whole century?"

"Maybe, maybe not. I believe I have to make a trip to Moosehead Hospital and talk to Sam Morrison. We need to find out how long the unit has been rented and by whom."

"Sage! Are you with the Sheriff?" Cliff yelled from the first floor. "Are you okay?"

"Come on up. We're in my bedroom," Sage replied. "Don't step in the blood on the stairs."

"Whose blood is that?" Cliff asked as he entered the bedroom expecting the worst.

"Relax. It's not your girlfriend's," the sheriff answered. "She put a world of hurt on Mr. Auction Man when he tried to steal her chair."

"Check this out," Sage said, pointing to the diamonds while trying to ignore the sheriff's choice of words.

"I guess we know why he was so persistent in coming after what he wanted. That's quite the pile of diamonds," Cliff said, pushing them around with his finger. "The question is, how did he know they were there?"

"That's the million-dollar question," the sheriff replied.

"I don't want him to know we found the diamonds. I'm going to tie the box, minus the diamonds, back onto the frame so if he breaks in tomorrow, he'll take the chair and disappear."

"I can put the diamonds in the safe at the farm if you want to get them out of your house. That is unless the sheriff thinks they should go to the police station," Cliff offered.

"The farm safe is a good idea. You can keep them hidden there until we find out who owns the unit and possibly the diamonds. Personally, I think the current owner of the unit had no idea they were there," the sheriff said.

"And we return to the same question. How did our suspect know they were there?" Sage replied.

"Hopefully, I'll get some answers tomorrow in Moosehead. And now that Cliff is here, I can go home and eat my supper. Before I go, I need to go out to my car and get an evidence bag to collect a sample of the blood that was left on the stairs. Let's keep the diamonds a secret for now. We don't need everyone and their brother coming out of the woodwork claiming them. I'll be in touch."

"These are amazing," Cliff said after the sheriff left. "Just think, there is a chance that you will own these. Did you ever imagine when you bought the unit it would contain something like this?"

"Not in a million years. Before I can even think about them belonging to me, we have to find out who owned the unit and if possible, the chair. Sheriff White said the diamonds are over a hundred years old, so we can only guess how long they have been hidden in the chair," Sage said, replacing the empty satchel in the little box. "This wingback chair dates to about the same time. It's not a reproduction; it's an original dating back to the Victorian era."

"Let me hold the flashlight over the hole so you can see what you're doing," Cliff offered.

"Now how can I cover the hole I cut so if he does come here tomorrow and tips the chair over, he won't be able to tell I found the diamonds?"

"I don't think it will matter much. If no one is here, he will rip the chair apart on the spot looking for the diamonds. He'll know as soon as he opens the box and finds it empty that you discovered them already."

"Let's make it a little harder on him. Will you move the chair to the storage trailer for me, please? If he's watching, he'll see the chair being moved out of the house, and I'd rather he break into my storage area than my house when I'm not here," Sage replied.

"Just prepare yourself. He may end up in the house anyway looking for the missing diamonds," Cliff said.

"Then it's a good thing you're taking them to the farm," Sage said. "I need to go downstairs and get an envelope. We can keep the diamonds all together, and you can stick them in your jean pocket and walk out in the morning without anyone knowing you have them."

"I have to agree with the sheriff, and I wouldn't tell anyone about the diamonds just yet," Cliff advised as he picked up the chair. "My dad is the only one who has access to the safe besides myself so I will have to tell him about the diamonds being secured in there. I know he won't like it, but we will need to keep them a secret from my mom."

"Tell him it's for her safety that she doesn't know they are there."

"Good idea," Cliff said, turning the chair to get it through the doorway.

While Cliff loaded the chair into the trailer, Sage stood at the bottom of the stairs trying to figure out the best way to clean up the blood. Thank goodness the stairs were all wood with no carpeting and would clean up easier.

Returning with a bucket of hot water mixed with ammonia, rubber gloves, and a mask, she started to wash down the stairs from the bottom to the top. Cliff returned and chatted with her while she cleaned. He suggested they go to the diner for supper after she was done and not worry about cooking supper. It served dinner until ten o'clock, and they had plenty of time to get there.

After the initial wash, Sage returned with a bucket of clean hot water mixed with pine cleaner for a final rinse. This time she worked from top to bottom to give the stairs time to dry, and she wouldn't be walking on them and leaving footprints.

The couple walked around checking the rest of the house for any other red spots left by the intruder. Satisfied they had gotten it all, Sage washed her hands, and they left for the diner.

Claire Marks, the owner of the diner met them at the door as they entered. She picked up a couple of menus and led them to a booth at the back out on the patio.

"Isn't Benny Finn your cousin?" Claire asked Sage.

"Yeah, on my dad's side. He moved away over ten years ago," Sage replied.

"He's back, and he's sitting in the corner over there. He's married now and introduced his wife as Nancy. I'll be back for your order."

"After we order, I'll go say hello to my cousin. I don't really know him that well as I wasn't close to anyone on my dad's side," Sage said, picking up the menu. "I feel like eating something different tonight."

As the couple looked over their menus, Benny came looking for Sage. Claire must have told him she was out on the patio, and he made the first move to get reacquainted.

"Sage! Long time no see," he said, reaching in for a hug. "How have you been?"

"Good. This is Cliff Fulton," she said, introducing her dinner companion.

"I remember you. Didn't you play basketball for Meadows Falls?" Cliff asked, shaking his hand.

"I did. And you played for Cupston. We played against each other our senior year for States."

"If I remember correctly, we beat you by two points at the buzzer," Cliff replied.

"That was the most heartbreaking game of my high school career," Benny said. "How's Sarah doing?"

"She's doing well. She hasn't changed at all and still owns and is working at *This and That*. What have you been up to? Claire says you got married?"

"Her name is Nancy. We met when my mom passed, and we had to put her house up for sale. Nancy is an independent real estate agent and runs her own agency. We just got married about a month ago."

"Still newlyweds," Sage said, smiling. "What brings you back to this area?"

"We were living in Meadows Falls right down the street from your dad. Nancy was doing really well until one of the big-name real estate chains moved into the area and took it over. So we decided to come to Cupston and check out the possibilities of her setting up a new office here. There's only one other agent listing properties locally, and she lives in Moosehead."

"Good luck to her. I hope things work out for both of you," Sage replied.

"Do you think Aunt Sarah would mind if I stopped in and visited her at the shop?"

"She's not there tomorrow but after that I don't see why not," Sage answered.

"Good! It will be nice to see my family members again even if it was only by marriage. I'll let you get back to eating. See you soon, and Cliff it was good to see you again."

"Well, that was out of the blue," Sage said. "I think my mom will be even more shocked to see him. My dad's family has basically ignored her since the divorce."

"Do you know what you want to order?" Claire asked, approaching their table. "The chicken cacciatore is excellent tonight."

"That's what I'll have," Cliff said, closing his menu.

"Sage?"

"I'm going to go with the fried chicken and waffles, with extra maple syrup, please."

"Cliff, you get a house salad with your meal. What kind of dressing would you like?"

"I like your homemade raspberry vinaigrette. I'll have that, please."

"Two iced teas?"

They both nodded as Claire picked up the menus and left the table. As they ate, they tried to piece together how the suspect knew about the hidden diamonds that were now safely secreted in Cliff's pants pocket. He had to be related to the storage unit's owner somehow. Sage was hoping that the sheriff would get some much-needed information when he went to visit Moosehead the next day.

Returning home, the house was as they had left it. Sage made up the couch for Cliff since he insisted he stay downstairs for the night. They both retired, knowing they had to be somewhere early in the morning.

Cliff was already up and waiting for Sage to come downstairs.

"Wow! You're an early riser," Sage said, reaching for her travel mug and the already brewed coffee.

"Farm life, what can I say?"

"I'll be closing the shop at five tonight, and then I'll be home. Can I expect you for supper?"

"I should arrive here about the same time. I hope they catch this guy soon. I can't stay here the following night as I have to be in Portland for a meeting and won't get back to Cupston until well after midnight."

"I'll be okay. I do appreciate you staying here while you can," she said.

"I can't let anything happen to you. Who would I date?" he asked, smiling.

"Lots of women want to date you," Sage said.

"Ahh, but I don't want to date other woman. I only want to date you," he said. "In fact, I'd like to call you my girlfriend if that's okay?"

"I wanted to take this slow," Sage said. "This dating thing has been a huge step for me, and it's not that I wouldn't like to be your girlfriend sometime down the road, just not right now. Are you upset with me?"

"No, not in the least. Just don't be surprised if more people start saying that just like the sheriff did," Cliff replied. "We do spend a lot of time together."

"Oh, you heard him say that, too?" Sage asked, slightly blushing.

"I did, and I felt kind of proud when he said it."

Sage didn't know how to respond. She liked spending time with Cliff but didn't want to be tied down just yet. Maybe it was her fear factor of relationships kicking in, but she had to listen to her gut instinct and not give in until she was ready to and felt comfortable doing so.

"I have to get going if I'm going to open my mom's shop on time," Sage said, trying to change the subject. "Do you need any more coffee? There is some left."

"I'm good. I already had two cups before you even got out of bed," he said as Sage turned off the coffee maker. "I'll see you tonight."

Sage watched him walk down the driveway to his truck. She knew it wasn't what he wanted to hear, but she had to be honest with him. He drove away with a wave. Locking the house and checking the workshop to make sure it was locked and the alarm was set, she left for *This and That.*

It was seven forty-five when she pulled into the parking lot of her mom's shop. She realized there had already been an early delivery when she noticed a box on the front steps. Exiting her van, she waved to

Flora and Paul who were having coffee on their front porch.

Flora is a totally different person now that she's out from under her brother's thumb. And her fiancé seems to be really nice, too.

Sage neared the box on the steps, and it appeared to move. Was her mind playing tricks on her, or did it really move? Then she heard a faint noise coming from the box as it moved again. No, it wasn't her imagination. She approached the box with caution.

CHAPTER FOUR

Written in black marker across the top of the box was a clear request that was being asked of her mom.

"Sarah, please take care of my babies. They are sweet and lovable and will give you hours of joy," Sage read out loud. "I can no longer keep them due to factors beyond my control. Please keep them together as they have never been apart."

She set down her coffee mug and opened the top of the box. Inside were two small kittens huddled in the corner. They looked up at Sage with big eyes and let out simultaneous meows. They were both grey, and one had a small white dot on the top of its head. They couldn't have been any more than six to eight weeks old.

I better call my mom, even though I don't like to bother her on her day off.

Sage unlocked the door, brought the box inside, and set it on the floor behind the register counter. She went to the refrigerator in the break room to see if her mom had any milk in there so that she could feed the kittens. There was some that Sarah used for her coffee. Sage grabbed a shallow bowl from the shelf next to the fridge and returned to the box.

She set the bowl in the box, but the kittens did not leave their corner. Sage picked each one up and set it at the edge of the bowl. Dipping her finger in the milk and softly rubbing the liquid on each kitten's mouth she watched until they realized it was something to eat. The smaller one decided to stand with his front two paws in the bowl as he ate.

"Mom, I hate to bother you on your day off, but you really need to come to the shop," Sage said when Sarah answered the phone.

"Is there something wrong?"

"No, it's just you got a delivery today that you need to see," Sage replied.

"I didn't have any deliveries scheduled for today."

"I figured as much. Please come to the shop when you can," Sage said.

"Okay. I'll be there in an hour or so," Sarah said, hanging up.

The kittens couldn't climb out of the box because it was too deep, so Sage knew she was safe to go about her routine to open up the shop. After putting the money in the register, she peeked in the box to see the two babies cleaning themselves in the corner after finishing eating.

They'll be asleep before too long.

Several customers visited the shop and never knew the kittens were behind the register. Sage sat on the stool and ate her midmorning snack when her mom showed up.

"What is so important to come to the shop on my day off? You know I have lots to do and only one day to get it done," Sarah said.

"Look behind me in the box," Sage replied.

She walked over and saw the two kittens asleep in the corner.

"Oh, dear," she sighed.

"Do you know who left them here?"

"I'm afraid I do. Another local confided in me that she was having problems in her marriage, and she would be leaving her husband. The only place she could find to stay right now was a hotel, and she couldn't take the kittens with her since they didn't allow pets."

"Did you offer to take them?" Sage asked.

"Not really, but I did offer to help her in any way I could. She probably figured if she left them with me, I'd take care of them and not turn them away," Sarah said, patting one of the kittens that had woken up and was meowing. "She knows I love animals."

"You already have three older cats. Will they be okay with kittens around?"

"I don't know. They're pretty set in their ways," Sarah said, frowning.

"Do you think it's permanent or just until she gets things straightened out and finds a place to live?"

"I don't know. It could be either. She mentioned that she might have to return to her mother's house to live until she can put some money away for her own place. And her mother is allergic to cats."

"Sounds like it could be permanent housing to me," Sage said, smiling at the two kittens who were now rolling around wrestling with each other.

"I think you're right."

"What are you going to do?"

"I don't know," Sarah admitted.

"I have a big house, and I'm home quite a bit. I could take them," Sage offered.

"Really? That would be so great. I don't want to see them go to the rescue league in case she can take them back."

"I could consider myself a foster until this person knows what is happening in her life. If she can't take them in the future, they would have a home with me."

"A chip off the old block," her mom said, hugging her. "I'm on my way to the grocery store. As a thank you I'll pick you up everything you need for the kittens, and I'll drop it off on my way back home. That way you'll have it at your house tonight and won't have to stop at the store."

"That sounds like a deal since I've never had any pets before and wouldn't know what to buy to start off," Sage said. "They are cute little fluffballs, aren't they?"

"They are indeed," Sarah said, peering into the box.

Flora walked in the front door. She saw her boss arrive and knew it was her day off and was making sure everything was okay at the shop.

"My daughter has new roommates," Sarah announced, pointing at the box.

"Is that what the people in the car left on the front steps this morning?" Flora asked.

"You saw them?" Sage asked.

"I saw her. A young woman placed the box on the step and returned to her car. She sat behind the wheel crying and then left. I didn't know who she was though, and I've never seen her in the shop before."

"The situation has been handled but thank you for watching over the shop for me while I'm not here," Sarah said to Flora. "You're a good friend."

"I have to protect my place of employment, don't you know. I love this job and the people who shop here," Flora said, smiling.

"Okay. I'm going shopping and will talk to you a little later," Sarah said to her daughter. "Walk me out, will you please, Flora."

Sage got into her cleaning routine. Periodically she would stop and play with the kittens. She was holding both of them in her lap when her mother returned with the needed necessities for Sage's new house guests. The grocery bags were loaded into the van and Sarah left.

A little past five, Sage flipped the sign on the door to closed, cleaned out the register and reset it for the next day. She hid the deposit bag in its normal hiding place in the fake potted plant, picked up the box the kittens were in and locked the front door.

Cliff was waiting in the driveway with the sheriff when she pulled in. Sage knew this couldn't be good if the sheriff was there. She left the kittens in the van and walked over to find out what was going on.

"He came for the chair, didn't he?" Sage asked.

"He came okay. The kitchen door had been jimmied open, and he went through the house looking for it. He broke into your trailer, found that the diamonds were missing and smashed the chair to pieces, I'm assuming out of anger," the sheriff replied.

"They are safe and hidden away where we discussed they would be put," Cliff said.

"I'm glad for that, but now I'm afraid his attention is going to shift from the chair to Sage because he thinks you have the diamonds now."

"Can the door be locked, or is there too much damage to it?" Sage asked.

"I think the whole door is going to have to be replaced," Cliff answered. "We can block it off for tonight, and I'll be on the couch so I can hear if someone messes with it during the night."

"I have quite a few doors in the storage trailer. Hopefully, I have one with the right dimensions and can change out the door tomorrow," Sage said.

"I'll help before I leave for my meeting in Portland," Cliff offered.

"I know I always say this to you, but please be

extra careful while you are here by yourself," Sheriff White said.

"I'll be home all day tomorrow and am going to be working out in my workshop just like I do every day. I don't want him to think anything has changed in case he's watching me," Sage said. "There is a possibility that he thinks that someone else found the diamonds before the chair was put in the unit."

"Could be but I wouldn't count on it," the sheriff said.

"Did you get any useful information in Moosehead today?" Sage asked.

"The unit belonged to an older woman named Nellie Fleming. The unit had been paid for up front for a year in advance when Nellie had to move into an assisted living facility and had no family to help her move her household goods to her new place. She told Sam when she signed for the unit that she would send someone to empty it once she was settled in and could find a moving company to do it."

"And the contents sat there for a whole year?" Cliff asked.

"They did. At the end of the year Sam tried to get a hold of Nellie at the address she had listed for the facility but was informed that she had developed dementia rather suddenly and passed. He waited for the legal three-month period and then listed the unit up for auction."

"I bet Nellie had no idea that the diamonds were hidden in her chair," Sage said.

"Or she was smart enough to know they would be protected where they were and figured she would retrieve them when her things were delivered to her new residence," the sheriff added.

"Or the dementia had already started to set in, and she forgot about them all together," Cliff replied.

"I think tomorrow I will have to do some online research on Nellie Fleming," Sage said. "Did Sam say where her house was that was sold?"

"She lived in Meadows Falls and moved to Moosehead Assisted Living Facility. Having no family or will, the bank took the house. It's a shame really as Nellie had been paying the mortgage even though she was at the facility. Maybe she hoped she would return to her home one day. There was less than a two-thousand-dollar balance left on the mort-gage when the bank reclaimed it."

"That's so sad," Sage said. "To be alone and have no one to guide you when you need it the most."

"They had a professional company come in and clean out the house, and it goes up for auction next month," the sheriff said.

"You might want to find out what company cleaned out the house. The cleaners might have found some paperwork that led them to the information about the diamonds and where they were hidden."

"Way ahead of you. I have one of my guys looking into it as we speak."

"Not to be creepy or anything, but the box on your front seat just moved by itself," Cliff said.

"The kittens! I forgot all about them," Sage said.

"Kittens?"

"Someone abandoned two kittens at my mom's shop this morning. She knows who left them there, but promised to keep the confidence that was entrusted to her. Mom already has three older cats, so I took the kittens home with me," Sage said, setting the box down in front of everyone.

"Cute," the sheriff said.

"I thought so. I couldn't stand the thought of them going to the rescue, so I took them. I have a big house they can play in, and they have each other for company so it was a no-brainer," she replied, reaching in and patting them. "The one with the white spot on his head has one of the loudest purrs I have ever heard."

"They don't have names?" Cliff asked.

"Not yet. I was going to work on that tonight," she said, smiling.

"I'm heading home to supper. Call me if you learn anything new," the sheriff said.

"I will," Sage replied.

"Supper will be a bit delayed. I have to get the kittens set up since they haven't had a litter box all day. And I need to see if they can eat wet food. I really don't know much about them I'm afraid."

"That's okay. I have some paperwork to finish up for my meeting tomorrow. Can I use the kitchen table?"

"Sure, go ahead."

Sage decided to put the litter box in the small spare room at the back of the house. She set it up and then brought the kittens to it to show them where it was. They used the box immediately and then walked around together checking out their new home. She set a plastic placemat on the floor in the corner of the kitchen and set down a plate of wet food and a dish of water on it. A short time later the kittens found it and between them cleaned the plate.

"Yow!" Cliff exclaimed.

Sage turned around to see the two kittens crawling up Cliff's leg. He reached down and pulled them off his leg and set them in his lap. They turned circles and settled down to clean themselves after eating. She could hear the cats purring as they fell asleep in Cliff's lap.

"It seems you have two new friends," Sage said, setting a salad on the table.

"What can I say? Animals and I are a thing," he replied, smiling.

"I forgot you had assorted animals on your farm."

"Not too many. A couple of goats, some sheep, and my mom's miniature Highland cow, Coo. We keep just enough animals around for the kids to pet while they visit the farm."

"Is Coo new?"

"Yeah, my mom has always wanted a Highland cow ever since she visited Scotland a few years ago. One was listed on a rescue site, and my parents went to get her. She's really cute and follows my mom everywhere."

"I'll have to come see her," Sage said. "Are you almost done with your paperwork? Supper is ready."

Cliff tried to gather his papers without disturbing the kittens. Sage picked them up and set them on the couch in her living room saying they shouldn't be at the table while people are eating.

"What are you going to call the kittens?" Cliff asked, putting some salad on each plate.

"Beer or wine?"

"Beer, please."

"I don't know. They both are solid grey with only a small spot of white separating them. They could be twins if it wasn't for that tiny difference. Any suggestions?"

"I don't know. Smokey and Spotty?"

"I like Smokey, but I'm not crazy about Spotty. How about Smokey and Motorboat?"

"Because of his loud purring? Clever," Cliff replied. "I like it."

"I guess they have been named," Sage said, sitting down with a plate of sticky, sweet chicken wings. "Dig in."

"I hope you have plenty of napkins," Cliff said, reaching for the wings.

The couple enjoyed a pleasant dinner together. After they ate, Sage was cleaning up the kitchen, and Cliff had returned to his paperwork when a loud crash sounded in the living room. Cliff grabbed the bat from the kitchen, and they both ran in the direction of the noise only to realize it was just the kittens who had knocked a plant out of the window.

Cliff lowered the bat, chuckling at the mess in front of them, relieved that it was only the cats.

"You find this amusing? That was the orchid my

grandmother gave me before she died. I hope it will be okay after I replant it," Sage said, picking up the plant, cradling it in her hands.

"I'm sorry. I'm chuckling at the fact that kittens will be kittens and get into all kinds of mischief. I think you need to kitten proof your house."

"The bay window will have to be first. They seem to like it there," Sage replied, watching Smokey and Motorboat wrestling on the shelf below the window. "They will probably lie there during the day in the warmth of the sunlight."

"Welcome to a world where pets dictate your life," Cliff said, smiling.

"Do you mind if I go to bed? It's been a long day, and I'm tired."

"No, go ahead. I'm going to finish my report and be right behind you."

"I need to leave the kittens downstairs, so they'll be close to the litter box. I hope they don't bother you too much during the night," Sage said.

"They won't. Good night."

Sage had just settled into bed and shut the light off when the window next to her bed exploded. She jumped out of bed, which was a mistake because she stepped on the broken glass. Falling back on the bed just as Cliff hit the doorway, she asked for a towel.

Cliff returned and gently wrapped her foot with the towel.

"You have shoes on. There's a rock with a note wrapped around it in the middle of the glass. Can you get it please?"

The note stated, *Return the diamonds or else.* Cliff laid the note and the rock on top of Sage's bureau and pulled out his cell phone.

"Return the diamonds? To whom? Is this guy serious?" Sage asked.

"I think we need to take you to the emergency room to have them remove the glass from your foot. One piece is pretty large, and it might require stitches when removed."

"We have to cover the window first. I don't need a gazillion mosquitoes in my house," Sage replied. "There's a roll of plastic down in the den that I use to cover the floor when I paint. Could you grab it for me? And the roll of duct tape out of the kitchen junk drawer."

Deputy Durst showed up as Cliff was taping the window closed. He took a quick report on the event and slid the note and the rock into a plastic evidence bag. He agreed with Cliff that Sage should go have her foot looked at.

"Don't tell anyone how this happened," Sage said

to Cliff as they went through the door at the emergency room. "If anyone asks, just say I accidentally put a broom handle through a window and then stepped in the glass."

"In other words, you're a real klutz," Cliff replied.

"Not funny, Fulton," Sage said as he gently set her down in a wheelchair that was just inside the entrance door.

Two hours later, they were back home, and Sage had six stitches in her foot. Her foot was wrapped, and the doctor had given her crutches to make sure she kept the weight off the foot while it healed. The kittens greeted them at the door meowing loudly.

Cliff got her situated on the couch and excused himself to make a phone call. Smokey jumped up on the couch and settled down next to her leg. Motorboat was not far behind and had jumped up on her shoulder, nestling himself under her hair.

"So, I just finished talking to my dad. He's going to the meeting tomorrow in Portland, and I'm staying here with you. This guy is a nut, and I don't want you alone at night while he's on the loose."

"You don't have to do that. I'll be fine," Sage insisted.

"No, my parents agree with me. I'll be staying here until this is over," Cliff said.

"I have to admit, I do feel safer with you here, and now with this stupid foot, I can't move as fast as I usually can."

"You sit right there with the cats. I'm going upstairs to sweep up the broken glass in your room. With my dad going to Portland, I'll have to do the harvesting tomorrow for the stand which means I'll be gone a good portion of the day. But I will be here by supper."

Cliff came down from upstairs, and in the short time he'd been sweeping, Sage had fallen asleep on the couch. He put a blanket over her and settled himself in the recliner next to her. He watched Smokey and Motorboat snuggle in with each other at Sage's side on the blanket.

The sun shone through the bay window, waking up Sage as the warmth covered her face. Cliff had already left for the farm. She hobbled to the coffee maker and brewed up a pot. The kittens meowed loudly, demanding to be fed.

"Is this how it's going to be every morning?" she asked the kittens. "Hold your horses, it's coming."

Sage grabbed her laptop from the living room, sat down with her cup of coffee, and checked her online sales since she hadn't been on the site for a few days. There were two sales that would have to be mailed out within the next few days. Moving on to her favorite search site, she plugged in the name Nellie Fleming to see what would pop up.

"Oh, this is going to be easy," she said sarcastically, seeing there were over four thousand Nellie Flemings listed. "Let's see if adding living in Meadows Falls whittles it down at all."

The new screen popped up.

"Bingo! I found you, Nellie Fleming."

Sage read on.

Nellie Fleming, born January 1, 1930, in Quincy, Massachusetts. Never married and no children. Two older brothers, Stanley and Floyd, were also born in Quincy. She worked at the North Quincy Post Office for forty years before retiring and moving to Meadows Falls, Maine.

"It seems like Nellie had a normal life. Nothing that stands out or too exciting," Sage said to the kittens as she got up to refill her coffee mug.

She sat down and continued to read. It was then she saw a newspaper story involving the brothers and clicked on the link.

Two Fleming Brothers Suspected in Jewel Heist in Boston: Stanley and Floyd Fleming of Quincy Massachusetts have been held and questioned in the heist that took place Friday, July 3, 1959, at the Diamond

Exchange in Boston. Four masked men held up the armored car before the guards could enter the building. The brothers were questioned and released for lack of evidence. The diamonds and pieces of jewelry have never been recovered.

"I need to send this link to the sheriff," Sage said.

After sending the link, she entered a search for the Diamond Exchange in Boston. The business had gone under in 1960, right after the heist, never being able to recover from the loss.

"So the brothers were in on it and hid the diamonds in their sister's house. But why didn't they retrieve them?" Sage asked Motorboat who had crawled up her leg and into her lap.

She kept scrolling. Several minutes later, she had her answer. Not even a month later, the brothers, involved in another robbery, were being chased by the police and crashed their car into a tree when they lost control of it. Both were killed instantly.

"Well, that explains why the diamonds were still there. But that means that the only other person that could have known about them would have been Nellie. Maybe she said something to someone as her dementia set in. This is so confusing," Sage said, getting up and washing her coffee mug and setting it in the strainer.

The kittens followed her in the bathroom and sat on the toilet watching her brush her teeth and wash her face. She put one sneaker on and a sock over the wrapped foot to keep the bandage clean.

"I'm going to *This and That* to see my mother. You two behave, and if anyone breaks into the house while I'm gone, you run and hide, got it? I won't be gone long."

Listen to me. Like they understand what I'm saying.

She packed up the jewelry from the storage unit and left for her mom's shop. The shop was busy. Flora was running around helping people while Sarah worked at the register. Sage limped to the counter.

"What did you to do your foot?" her mom asked.

Sage told her mom what happened the night before and the stupid way she injured her foot. Then she told her she had some jewelry for her to look at and where the jewelry had come from. Her mother promised to check it out when things slowed down. She told her daughter to put it in the top drawer of the desk in the office.

"Aunt Sarah?"

Sage turned around recognizing the voice. Benny stood there with a woman that Sage had never seen before, yet the woman acted like she recognized her.

She quickly turned and stared into a case full of antique books.

"Benny Finn? As I live and breathe, it is you, isn't it?" his aunt said, coming out from behind the register.

"Hello, Aunt Sarah. How have you been?" he said, hugging her back.

"You are the last person I thought would come walking into my shop. Sage, do you remember your cousin Benny?"

"I do and I already saw him at the diner."

"His name is Ben, not Benny," the woman with him said nastily, keeping her back to everyone. "Benny is a name you use for a child not a grown man."

"Lighten up, will you? They're my family, and to them, I have always been Benny. Aunt Sarah, Sage, this is my wife, Nancy."

"Are you almost done here? I have a long list of things I have to get done today," she said, ignoring everyone there.

"Nice to meet you, too," Sage snarled back at the rude woman.

Nancy glared at Sage, her eyes narrowed, and her lips pressed together so hard they were turning white.

"I'll be in the car. Hurry up, will you?" Nancy

said, storming to the door and crashing into Flora on her way out. She blew out the door without even apologizing to her.

"I am so sorry for the way my wife acted. She has a lot on her plate right now losing her business in Meadows Falls and having to start over again here in Cupston."

"You'd think she would want some friends around here if she's starting a new business," Sage replied. "With her lousy attitude, she won't get many clients here in Cupston."

"Sage! Really," her mom said.

"What? I say it like it is, and I always have," Sage mumbled.

"It's okay, Aunt Sarah. My cousin is right. Her attitude does need some adjusting. It's just her brother is pressuring her to get the real estate office up and running because his business is tied to hers. His company goes in and cleans out the houses before they go onto the market. He has four guys who work for him who aren't getting a paycheck right now, and that is weighing heavy on Nancy."

"I'm sorry for her troubles," she said, heading back to the register to ring up a customer's purchases. "Do you want us to call you Ben from now on and not Benny?"

"Either one is fine with me," he replied. "We're staying in a rental house here in town over near the park. I guess I'll head out before she comes back in and causes a scene. Is it okay if I stop by again to visit when I don't have Nancy with me?"

"I would love that," Sarah replied. "You stop by anytime."

Sage walked to the front window and watched as her cousin and his wife pulled away. The more she thought about it, she had seen Nancy somewhere before, but where?

"What's bothering you?" Sarah asked, walking up behind her.

"I have seen her somewhere before, and I know she realized it. Did you see her look at me and then quickly turn away?"

"I don't understand how our Benny ended up with someone like her. He's so easygoing and pleasant. Love, I guess you can't explain it," her mom said. "Speaking of love, how's it going with you and Cliff? I hear he's staying at your house to protect you from the bad guys."

"He's sleeping down on the couch, Mom. We are still just friends, for now anyway."

"I'm glad you said for now. It gives me a little

hope that maybe I'll be planning a wedding before I'm put in a nursing home," Sarah said, smiling.

"Mom, you're impossible," Sage replied, hugging her.

"Back to work for me. The customers are piling up at the register. Will I see you at bingo this weekend?"

"I'll be there. See you then. Call me if you get a chance to look at the jewelry. I want you to sell it here at the shop if you think it's worth it."

Sage checked her house when she got home looking for break-ins. Everything appeared normal and untouched. The kittens followed her around, meowing to her, like she had been gone for a year. She picked them up and patted each one. Satisfied, they ran off chasing each other up and down the hall-way. Locking the door to the house, she went to her workshop to get some things done.

First on the list was to snap a picture on her cell phone of each painting so she could research the painter and its history when she returned inside for lunch. She then laid each one down flat and reglued the paper backings. Leaving them to dry, she moved on to her next project.

A dry sink that was in pretty bad shape and missing one of its front doors was going to be turned into a bar. She removed the hinges that were holding the remaining door on the piece. Next she took her favorite jigsaw and carefully cut off the top section of the sink. The top section would be added to and reattached to give the top of the sink some height for storing liquor bottles.

Her cell phone rang.

"Hello."

"Sage, you need to come to the shop immediately. Your mom is missing and the note, oh my, the note," Flora babbled into the phone.

"What do you mean she's missing? What note?" Sage asked.

"It's bad, really bad," Flora mumbled.

"Have you called the sheriff?"

"I did, and he's on his way. Hurry, please."

CHAPTER FIVE

Sage broke all the posted speed limits to get to *This and That*. The sheriff was already there along with Deputy Bell. They had sent the remaining customers away and secured the crime scene.

"Where's my mom?" Sage asked, limping toward the group.

"I told you this man was dangerous. This isn't good, Sage," Sheriff White replied. "Read this."

She walked to the register where the sheriff was standing and scanned the note. It said that Sage had something they wanted, and now they had something she wanted. They would be in touch to arrange an exchange.

"Flora, how did they get her while you were in the shop?" Sage asked.

"I went home for lunch to spend an hour with Paul. He's home working on paperwork for one of his cases, and I went to make him some lunch. When I came back the front door was wide open, and Sarah was gone."

"That means they were sitting close by watching the shop," Sage surmised.

"At first, I thought she might have gone out to one of the storage areas because we have a lot of holes to fill on the shelves. But I still couldn't find her when I went out to check."

"Where and when did you find the note?" the sheriff asked.

"I went to ring up a customer, and the note was propped up on the front of the register. It was then I knew there was a reason Sarah wasn't answering my calls. I called the sheriff right away. Oh, why did I go home for lunch? She'd probably still be here if I had stayed put."

"It's not your fault, Flora. They might have taken you, too, and then we'd have two people to worry about," Sage said, wrapping an arm around the shoulders of the distraught woman.

"Did you touch the note, Flora?"

"No, sir. I've read enough crime books to know better."

"Bell, glove up and put the letter in an evidence bag. Maybe we can get a fingerprint off it," the sheriff said. "Get it back to the lab and tell them to put a rush on it."

"What do I do?" Sage asked the sheriff. "We know what they want. If I give them the diamonds, will they return my mom alive?"

"I received the link you sent me, and I have a friend of mine on the Boston force looking into the robbery. The question still remains, how do these people know about the diamonds?"

"What diamonds?" Flora asked. "They took Sarah for some diamonds?"

"Yes, they did, but no one can know that. It has to be kept a secret, Flora, or we may never get my mom back."

"I won't say a word, I promise."

"The shop is going to remain closed for at least today while we get the crime unit in here to see if they can find anything useful to help us. Flora you can take the rest of the day off, but remember, don't say anything about the diamonds, not even to your fiancé," the sheriff said. "If anyone asks, you don't have a clue as to what is going on."

"I'll put the closed sign out at the opening of the parking lot," Sage said. "Flora, I will call you if the shop is going to be open tomorrow, but I highly doubt it will be."

"I'll put the sign up on my way out. You don't need to be dragging around a heavy sign with your foot the way it is," Bell said. "Just tell me where it is."

"Thanks, Andy. The sign is leaning up on the side of the shop."

After everyone was gone and it was just the sheriff and Sage in the shop, she started to cry. Sheriff White guided her to a chair and sat next to her. He offered her his handkerchief from his pocket.

"It hasn't been used; I swear. It's clean," he said, smiling.

"Thank you," she said, taking the handkerchief.

"I know you're worried, but if anyone can take care of themselves, it's Sarah. She is one feisty lady and won't let them get the better of her."

"I worry because of what he did to Sam at the storage facility," Sage replied. "What's to stop him from doing the same thing to my mom and leaving her somewhere to die even if he gets what he wants."

"That's exactly why we have to figure out who he is and how he found out about the diamonds. Somehow the connection will tell us where your mom is."

"I just hope we're in time."

"Do you have a key to this place? I know there's no alarm, even though I've tried to talk your mom into getting one for years."

"I do."

"Give the key to me so I can wait for the crime unit to get here. I'll lock up the shop when they're done and drop the key off at your place on my way home. And I want you to leave the diamonds right where they are for now. Don't play the hero and bring them to your house. Call me if they get in touch with you about the exchange."

"I'm going home to do a deep dive on my computer on Nellie Fleming. There has to be something I am missing," Sage said. "I'll return your handkerchief after I wash it."

"The crime unit is here. Head home and make sure you lock the doors behind you," he said. "I'll be over later."

Several cars pulled up out front when Sage was on her way out. They were there to shop and didn't understand why the shop was closed. She told them that a family emergency had arisen and that she wasn't sure when the store would open again. They offered to help in any way they could before they drove off.

At home, Sage found the two kittens sleeping in the warm sunlight coming in through the bay window. They opened their eyes and stretched when she entered the living room but didn't get up.

"Aren't you just the comfortable ones?" she said to the kittens. "I wish I knew if my mom was comfortable."

She grabbed her computer, a notebook and pen, and a glass of root beer. Settling on the couch, she crossed her legs and balanced the computer across her lap and went to work. She returned to the site that she had bookmarked and continued to read about Nellie Fleming's life.

Her cell phone kept going off, but the only one of importance was from Cliff. The sheriff had stopped by the farm and told him what had happened to Sarah. He also told him that the diamonds should be kept where they were until the exchange was arranged. The sheriff didn't like to go behind Sage's back, but he was afraid she would panic and go do something on her own if she had the gems in her possession. Cliff agreed.

He asked her if she wanted him to come to the house with her but she knew his dad had gone to Portland so she told him she would be okay. She was staying in the house with the doors locked and working on her computer. Cliff said he would see her around six.

For several hours, Sage continued to click on links that had anything to do with the Fleming family. Most of the articles were repeats of information she had already read. She sat back, closed her eyes, and gave her brain a moment to rest. Then it hit her. She was going about her search all wrong.

If the brothers had died and Nellie was the only one who knew about the diamonds, it would only stand to reason that she had written something down about them and the information would have been kept in her house. Maybe she hid the diamonds in the chair and not the brothers. Sam told the sheriff that Nellie had every intention of bringing her things to the assisted living facility as soon as she could find someone to move them, but she never got a chance to clean out the storage unit because her health failed so quickly.

She had no family to go through her things when she died which left only one conclusion. Whoever cleaned out what was left in the house had full access to information about the existence of the diamonds. Now Sage had a new direction in her search. Her main goal was to find out who the bank used to clean out the house before it went to auction, and what agent they used to run the auction of the property.

Sage decided to go directly to the source to find out the name of the bank. She had the street address in Meadows Falls so she did a reverse search looking for the new owners' names and their telephone number. When she called them, she told them that she had come into possession of some of Nellie Fleming's property and wanted to know which bank had sold her house, figuring they would have records of anyone related to her.

They told her that they bought the house, at auction, from the Meadows Falls Credit Union. Sage asked the man if anyone else had been interested in the house and maybe even a little aggressive in their bidding. The new owner said no and that only three people had actually shown up for the auction as the house was older and needed a lot of work. Sage thanked them for their help and hung up.

They didn't bid on the house, which meant they already had the information they needed and knew the diamonds were in the chair in the storage unit. This narrows the field down even more to the company that cleaned out the house. Now to call the bank and see if they will tell me the name of the company they use.

Sage was transferred to the customer service rep

who was extremely helpful. She told her they used the same company out of Portland named High Point Auction House for all their clean outs. They had a good reputation and had never had a complaint lodged against them in all the work they had done for the bank. The rep also told her the bank used their own personnel to conduct the auctions, so that was a dead end for Sage.

She returned to the computer and typed High Point Auction House in the search bar. The web page was impressive. They had been in business for fifteen years and had many five-star reviews listed on the jobs they had completed. The owner's name was Peter Graziano. She searched the pictures on the website and found one of the five-man crew emptying a house. Sage clicked on the picture to enlarge it.

"Got you!" she yelled, scaring the kittens who were lying on the couch next to her.

She picked up her phone to call the sheriff, but as she was about to dial, her phone rang. She didn't recognize the number, and usually, she didn't answer those kinds of calls, but something made her take the call.

"Hello."

"If you want to see your mother again, put the diamonds in a clear plastic bag and bring them to the

Cupston Gazebo at dusk. Leave them under the first stair and walk away. We will be watching you."

"I want to talk to my mom," Sage demanded angrily.

"You're not in a position to demand anything. She will be left somewhere in the park after we have the diamonds in our possession. Don't call the police. We won't call you again."

The call went dead.

"Don't call the sheriff, yeah right," she yelled at the phone. "I know who you are now."

"Sage, are you okay? I hear yelling," the sheriff said, standing at the screen door.

"Hold on," she said, unlocking the door. "I was just going to call you. I know who our suspect is and how he found out about the diamonds. Follow me. And they just called about the exchange, but they wouldn't let me talk to my mom."

"What do they want you to do?"

"They want the diamonds delivered to the gazebo in the park at dusk and set under the first stair. They said they would be watching me and that once they had the diamonds, they would release my mom somewhere in the park."

"I don't like it. There is no guarantee they will release Sarah when they get their hands on them."

"I was thinking the same thing. So we have to stay one step ahead of them and get to my mom before dusk sets in."

"You said you knew who the suspect is?"

"His name is Peter Graziano. He owns the High Point Auction House in Portland. His company cleaned out Nellie's house before it was auctioned off."

"That doesn't mean it was him just because he owns the company," the sheriff replied.

"No, but this picture does," she said, showing him the group picture and pointing to the man in the center. "This is the man who tried to outbid me at the auction for Nellie's unit."

The sheriff frowned.

"What are you thinking?" Sage asked.

"Portland is a bit far away. It makes sense that he would have to have somewhere local to hold your mom and be able to be all the places he has been showing up."

"I was thinking about that, too. And I hate to say this without any proof, but I think I know who's helping him and might be hiding him," Sage said.

"Who?"

"When my cousin Benny was in my mom's shop, he had his new wife with him. She was a piece of work, let me tell you. She was rude, and when she looked at me, it was almost like she recognized me from somewhere and wouldn't look in my direction again. She stormed out of the shop and sat in their car."

"And?"

"Benny tried to make an excuse for her bad behavior saying she was under a lot of pressure after losing her business. He also told us her brother's business was tied to hers. She had no current clients, and he had four men that worked for him that weren't getting a paycheck right now. Can you guess what his business was?"

"He cleans out houses?" the sheriff asked.

"Bingo. The boss and a four-man crew," she said, pointing to the computer screen.

"If it is her and her brother, your cousin could be in danger, too. Do you know where they are staying here in town?"

"The only thing Benny told me was they were staying in a rental house over near the park. And now that I think about it, what a perfect place to watch the gazebo from."

"There aren't too many rental properties over there. There's only three that I can think of offhand, and two of them are up in the woods. Both are pretty isolated."

"We have to get moving … oh geez. I just remembered where I saw Nancy. She was at the auction bidding against me for the unit. She had a kerchief over her hair and large sunglasses on. She quit bidding and left when her brother arrived."

"That's why she turned away from you at your mom's shop," the sheriff replied.

"Dusk is at seven fifty-two tonight," Sage said, checking her phone. "We need to check out those houses before the sun goes down."

"We?"

"You don't have enough deputies to check out all the properties at once. If they see you go into another house near them, they might take off, and then we'll never find my mom."

"Hello! Where is everyone?" Cliff yelled from the kitchen.

"Cliff is here. We can check one house while you and your deputies check out the other two," Sage said, volunteering Cliff's services.

"What am I getting volunteered for now?"

"We have a lead on where my mom might be," Sage replied.

"Your girlfriend here has discovered who our suspect is and where they might be staying locally.

The problem is I don't have enough manpower on hand to cover all the places we have to be at the same time," the sheriff said. "And we are running out of time because dusk is fast approaching, and that is when the diamonds are supposed to be delivered."

"Count me in. It enrages me that they took Sarah, and I'll do whatever it takes to help get her back," Cliff stated.

"I'm going to get my deputies together and we will meet at the Wilson's Ice Cream Stand in half an hour. Sage, I need you to get a plastic bag, break up some ice cubes so it looks like there are diamonds in the bag if they are indeed watching you. We will break up into teams of two and hit each house at the same time. Are you going to be okay walking around on your foot?"

"I'll be fine. I'll wrap another ace bandage around it before I leave and put a couple of socks on it. My foot comes in second to getting my mom back."

"Meeting at the ice cream stand is a good cover if they are watching you. It will look like we're out on a date," Cliff said, watching Sage wrap her foot. "Do you have a hammer inside the house so I can break up the ice cubes?"

"In the junk drawer next to the fridge. The plastic bags are in the bottom drawer."

Cliff smashed the cubes into smaller pieces, so they were diamond sized. He placed them into a fresh bag that had no marks on it from hitting it with the hammer.

"Looks like diamonds to me," Sage said, holding up the bag. "I'm going to wrap this in foil to keep it from melting too fast."

"Are we ready to go?" Cliff asked.

"Let's go find my mom."

At the ice cream stand, it was decided that the two teams of police would take the farthest houses into the woods, figuring it would be easier to hide someone there because it was more isolated. Sage and Cliff would approach the first house on the dirt road from the rear. If it got too close to dusk, Sage would circle back and approach the gazebo from the main road. Checking their watches, they agreed to meet back at the stand after they searched their perspective houses.

Sheriff White and Deputy Bell drove off in one unmarked car while Durst and Plummer followed in another. Cliff and Sage were close enough to the first house to walk on foot. Cliff bought them ice creams, and they leaned against the truck eating while perusing the area. They definitely looked like they were out on a date to anyone watching.

"Take my hand," Cliff said. "It will look like we

are out on a stroll as we head to the house. Leave the foil in the truck."

"You just want to hold my hand," Sage said, teasing him. "But whatever works."

They joined hands and strolled toward the dirt road eating their treats all the while looking behind trees and anywhere else where someone could be hiding. Ducking behind a large rock, they watched Benny stroll out of the rental house. Sage texted the sheriff that the first house was where they were staying. Her cousin got in his car and drove off.

"Let's look in the windows at the back of the house," Sage suggested.

The couple circled the house but saw no movement through the windows.

"Maybe they aren't keeping her here," Sage said, disappointed.

The sheriff pulled up.

"There's no one inside," Sage told him. "Benny just left, but he was alone."

"It's almost dusk. You should head back and put the fake diamonds under the gazebo. We'll watch from here to see who retrieves them."

"They are supposed to release my mom somewhere in the park once they have the diamonds," Sage said. "They didn't say where."

"I have Durst and Plummer staking out the other end of the park in case they drop her there," the sheriff said.

Sage did as instructed. She placed the bag of ice under the stairs of the gazebo, looked around, and then walked back to the ice cream stand. She and Cliff drove away, parking two streets over. Sage took out her binoculars to watch who showed up to pick up the package using two houses on the street as her cover.

Time passed, and no one came to pick up the diamonds. Sage was afraid that in the heat of the summer, the ice would be totally melted when they did finally show up. Through her binoculars, she could see couples milling around the gazebo, eating their ice cream, and maybe that was scaring the suspect away.

"Cliff," Sage cried out. "It's him."

Handing him the binoculars so he could see the suspect, Sage stood there in shock.

"That's not the guy you showed me on the computer," Cliff stated.

"I know. The sheriff will be looking for that guy, too. He won't be looking for my cousin Benny," Sage replied. "He doesn't even know my cousin, and it might be too late for the sheriff to react once Benny tries to pick up the diamonds and sees it is melted ice. I have to text him."

"Your cousin is behind this?"

"I don't know, maybe he is being forced to participate. For the life of me, I can't see him ever hurting my mom."

"He just reached for the bag and is extremely mad at what he found. He slammed the bag on the ground and took off running," Cliff said.

"Is he running toward the rental?" Sage asked.

"No, he's running toward the ice cream stand. Get in the truck so we can follow him," Cliff said. "The sheriff is coming from the other direction, so maybe we can pin him in."

The couple reached the end of the road and waited for Benny to drive by them, but he never appeared. The sheriff drove up, stopped in front of them, and leaned out his window.

"Did he come this way?"

"No, he didn't. We figured we could pin him in, but he didn't come this way," Cliff replied.

"That means he had to take the dirt road behind the stand. It was the only other way out, and he could be anywhere by now."

"He had to have scouted out the area previously to know that road leads out to the main road. Only locals would attempt to go down that road, it's so rough looking," Cliff said.

Sage sat quietly in the truck. The sheriff noticed.

"Durst, is there any sign of Sarah Fletcher on your end of the park?" the sheriff asked into his shoulder radio.

"Negative," he replied.

"That means he had no intention of releasing my mom. He still has her stashed somewhere if she's even still…" Sage choked out.

"Don't think like that. Let's go back to the rental house and see if we can figure out where he might have gone. We have probable cause to enter the house," the sheriff stated.

Bell was ready to bust in the front door, but to everyone's surprise the front door was unlocked and swung open. The house was quiet as they entered. The sheriff and Bell headed for the bedrooms while Sage and Cliff walked into the kitchen. A half-eaten sandwich was on the table along with an empty beer bottle.

"The bedrooms are empty," the sheriff said, returning to the kitchen.

"Shh," Sage said, moving to the front of what looked like a cellar door. "Listen. Someone's down there."

CHAPTER SIX

"Stay here," the sheriff ordered as he opened the door. "Bell, follow me."

He found the light at the top of the stairs, and they headed down, disappearing out of sight. Cliff and Sage could hear a muffled sound like a person who was gagged but trying to speak.

"Sage! Cliff! Can you come down here?"

When they hit the bottom of the stairs, they could see two people bound and gagged lying on a mattress on the dirt floor. They were trying to get themselves untied to no avail.

"I know who this guy is," the sheriff said. "Do you know this woman?"

"Her name is Nancy, and she is my cousin's

wife," Sage answered, tearing off her gag. "Where is Benny holding my mom?"

"That backstabbing traitor. He made us do all the dirty work and then he thought he could take off with the diamonds and leave us behind with nothing. And he's not really my husband. It was all a story we used to come back here and get to you."

"Where is my mom?" Sage demanded through gritted teeth, losing her patience with Nancy.

"Before I tell you, did he get his greedy hands on the diamonds?" Nancy replied.

"You are in no position to not be answering our questions," the sheriff warned. "Where is Sarah Fletcher?"

"More than likely, she's right where Benny put her in the first place. She's at my half-empty realty office in Meadows Falls. Now, did he get the diamonds or not?" Nancy asked.

"What is the name of the office?" the sheriff asked.

"Meadows Falls Realty on Main."

The sheriff whipped out his cell phone and put in a call to the Meadows Falls PD. He wanted them to get to Sarah before Benny had a chance to get back there and move her or something worse. They said they would call when they found her.

"How did you find out about the diamonds and where they were?" Sage asked.

"My brother cleaned out Nellie's house and found her daily journal. That woman wrote everything down. It's like she was writing a book or something."

"How did my cousin get involved?"

"Peter brought home the journal and showed it to me while we were eating. It was all Benny's idea to buy the storage unit and get the diamonds. No one would have ever known we had them. Then you had to come into the picture and buy the unit out from under us."

"We never meant for anyone to get hurt," Peter said when his gag was removed. "I've never been in trouble my whole life and neither has my sister."

"You never meant for anyone to get hurt? What do you call what happened to Sam Morrison at the storage facility?" the sheriff asked.

The siblings looked at each other like they had no idea what he was talking about.

"What happened at the facility? We were only there one day, and that was the day of the auction," Peter replied.

"Are you saying you didn't beat Sam Morrison to a pulp and dump him in the dumpster?" the sheriff asked.

"I never went back there, and I would never beat anyone up and leave them in a dumpster. It must have been Benny," Peter said. "I have a family, and if I knew the extremes that he would go to, I never would have gone along with his plan. I was just looking to score a little extra money."

"Who threw the rock through my window?" Sage asked.

"That was me, but in my defense, Benny was driving the car, and he threatened my family if I didn't do it," Peter said. "I should have known right then that if he threatened my family, he would double-cross us in the long run."

"We have Sarah Fletcher. She is on her way by ambulance to Moosehead Hospital to be checked out," a voice said over the sheriff's shoulder radio. "She is in good shape, and her only complaint is she's hungry."

"My mom's okay," Sage whispered, tearing up.

"Durst is outside with the cruiser to transport," Bell announced, coming down the stairs.

The duct tape around the prisoner's wrists were replaced with handcuffs. The siblings whispered between themselves.

"Hey, no talking," Bell said.

"We decided that we are not taking the brunt of

this and letting that scum get away. He had a ticket for Ireland leaving from Logan out of Boston on the red eye. He set us up and used us. We want him to pay," Nancy said.

"I'll call Boston PD and put them on alert so they can watch the airport for his arrival," the sheriff said. "Now, I think it's time for you two to go to Moose-head and see your mom."

"We need to run by the house and pick up my car. The three of us will not fit in the front seat of your truck," Sage said, smiling for the first time in many hours. "Let's go get my mom and bring her home."

The next morning, Sage called her mom to check on her only to find that she was at work like nothing had happened. Sage made the quick drive over to *This and That* since Sarah had something she had to tell her.

"Mom, what are doing at work? The doctor told you to take a few days and rest."

"I can rest perfectly fine here sitting on a stool at the register."

"She's right," agreed Flora. "I won't let her lift anything or move from that stool."

"She's worse than a prison warden," Sarah mumbled, sulking.

"I am," Flora said, walking away. "And don't you

forget it."

"They got your cousin trying to board a plane to Ireland at three this morning. He's in jail in Portland while he waits for his trial to begin, with no bond because they believe he is a flight risk. They want me to come testify against him," Sarah said.

"Are you going to do it?"

"Darn tootin' I am. He had a lot of nerve floating back into Cupston and into our lives fooling everyone the way he did."

"What is it you wanted to show me?" Sage asked, smiling at her mom's fierceness.

"Remember that jewelry you brought to me from the storage unit? I was examining it when Benny came into the shop. I don't know what made me do it, but I swept everything into the drawer and closed it before he saw it."

"And that was a good thing?"

"It sure was. These pieces are not costume jewelry. They are Victorian-era pieces that are authentic gold, diamonds and other gemstones."

"I wonder if these were the pieces that were stolen alongside the diamonds," Sage said. "I don't believe the pieces were listed and detailed individually so it would be hard to know if these were Nellie's or part of the theft."

"That is why I called the sheriff. He said he would call his friend and get back to me," her mom said. "Speaking of the devil."

"Good morning, Fletcher women. And how is Miss Sarah feeling today?"

"I am fine, thank you. And thank you again for finding me," Sarah said.

"It wasn't me that figured everything out, it was your daughter. She gets all the credit," the sheriff admitted.

"Am I to assume you found out something about the jewelry and that's why you're here?"

"I did. My friend in Boston has been doing some research on the robbery. It took place in 1959, and the diamond exchange went out of business in 1960. The insurance company, Black Swan Insurance, offered a reward for the return of the diamonds but not the jewelry. The reward expired in 2001 when the insurance company folded. Where there was no listing pertaining to the jewelry, there is no way to prove if they are the stolen pieces or not."

"So are you saying the jewelry is Sage's?" Sarah asked.

"That's what I'm saying," the sheriff said, smiling.

"What about the diamonds?" Sage asked.

"Whereas the robbery took place sixty-five years ago, and all the parties concerned have gone out of business or died, my colleague in Boston feels that the statute of limitations has passed, and you legally own the diamonds. You purchased a storage unit that they were in, and they belong to you. He does suggest that you lock them away in a bank deposit box for a year or so to make sure no one comes forward with a claim on them."

"That is such great news," Sarah said, hugging her daughter. "Security for your future."

"Maybe you can turn one of those diamonds into an engagement ring," the sheriff said, teasing Sage.

"I don't know about that," Sage said, turning bright red. "But what I do know is that Gabby is going to want to go buy storage units every weekend after this score."

"If I were you, I'd keep the diamond thing low key and just hide them away like my friend advised," the sheriff said.

"That might be hard to do. After all, this was the score of a lifetime for a flipper."

***

If you enjoyed Chair-Ish the Thought and are looking for more Trash to Treasure adventures, check out Mirrored in Murder, today!

Printed in Great Britain
by Amazon